The Emperor's Regret by Barbara A. Pierce.

ISBN 978-1-970072-32-7 (Paperback)
ISBN 978-1-970072-33-4 (Hardback)

This book is written to provide information and motivation to readers. Its purpose is not to render any type of psychological, legal, or professional advice of any kind. The content is the sole opinion and expression of the author, and not necessarily that of the publisher.

Printed in the United States of America.

New Leaf Media, LLC
175 S. 3rd Street, Suite 200
Columbus, OH 43215
www.thenewleafmedia.com

This book is dedicated to the following people:

Jean Hurst
Maz Hogan
Rita Patrick
Michael Yanis
Diamond Green
Frances Lightsy
Barbara Green
Marva Pierce
Vivian Randall
Frances Jones
Tracy Matthews
Lavinia Smith

Thanks to everyone who continues to support me in my efforts.

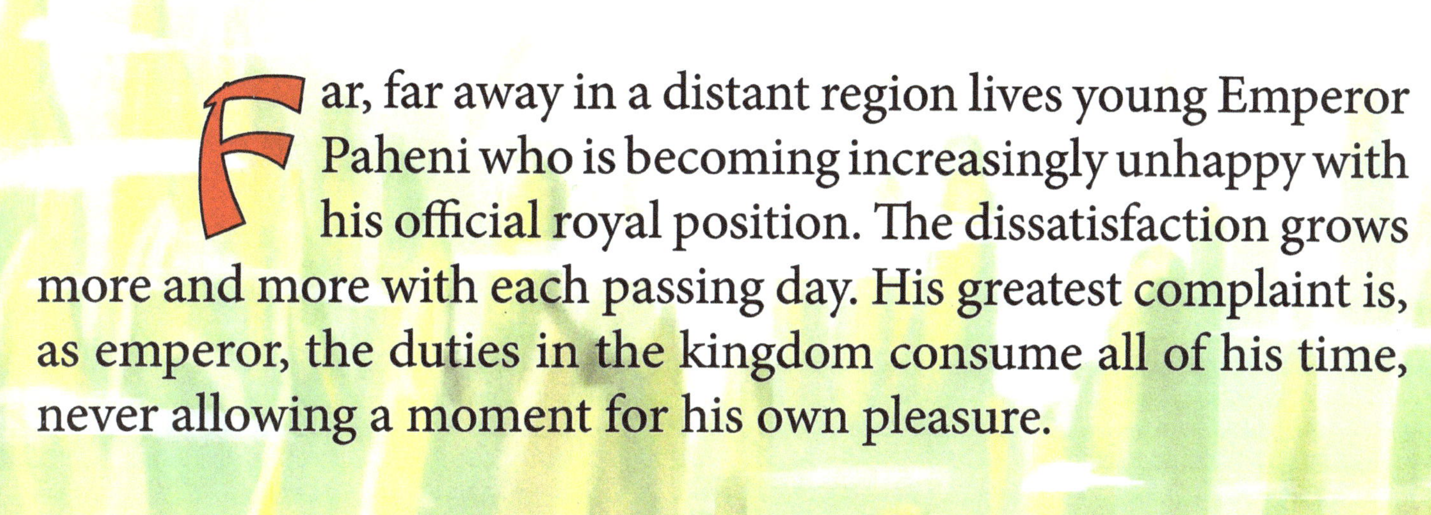

Far, far away in a distant region lives young Emperor Paheni who is becoming increasingly unhappy with his official royal position. The dissatisfaction grows more and more with each passing day. His greatest complaint is, as emperor, the duties in the kingdom consume all of his time, never allowing a moment for his own pleasure.

"Carrying out official responsibilities must be a priority for a sovereign ruler. There is little time for much frivolity in the life of a great emperor!" a statement often overheard during his childhood.

Of course, that was long before he inherited his father's throne.

Periodically, the young ruler tries to think of ways in which to bring about some real change in his life, but is never able to do so.

Finally, reaching his wit's end, Paheni, feeling he has to do more, summons Haknobee, one of his most trusted subjects, an aged man of great wisdom and one who is also known to possess powerful magic.

As soon as the man enters the royal chamber, the emperor immediately starts pouring out his feelings, hoping for a solution. "Is there anything you can think of that might possibly help to change my grievous lot in this life?" he asks.

Greatly surprised by what has just been revealed to him by the highest-ranking royal member, Haknobee says nothing for a moment. He appears to be deep in thought as he slowly rubs his balding head, then says, "Exalted One, I will need a day or two to think this through!"

The emperor grants the old gentleman permission to leave, but fears the worst. "What if something happens to him before he returns? My life will remain the same boring, routine-drudgery that it is now!" he says to himself.

The young man does not have to wait very long. Just a few hours later the elder returns filled with excitement. Upon entering the throne room he bows dutifully to Paheni, then quickly blurts out the solution he thinks will solve his dilemma. The man of great magic tells of a chance meeting he'd had with a parrot deep in the rainforest a few months earlier. Like Paheni, the bird had voiced how dissatisfied he was with his way of life in the wild.

s Haknobee speaks, the emperor's expression goes from that of interest to wide-eyed disbelief.

The suggestion that is made seems quite far-fetched to the emperor and he does not hesitate to say so.

"Have you forgotten who I really am, and what I can do?" the elder asks.

"I know you are very wise and are able to do great feats of magic, but what you are proposing now, sounds truly impossible!" says the young man.

The elder says in a stronger voice, "There are few things in the realm of magic beyond my powers!"

The young man gets excited thinking, maybe there is a possibility of breaking free of his royal responsibility! Could this little man really pull it off? That would certainly be a wonderful thing, just endless fun, and no official duties to perform!

The emperor, still excited about the prospect of being able to live a carefree life, begins to have second thoughts, but pushes them aside as they pop up.

Not wanting Haknobee to know how anxious he is, Paheni says he will get back to him, perhaps the following day.

That night there is neither sleep for the emperor, nor anyone else in his palace. When he isn't making requests of the servants, he is thinking how meaningless life is becoming for him, how overwhelming his responsibilities are, and that there must be something else much better.

In a loud outburst he says, "What good is having power, when it becomes a burden!" For the young man it seems like morning will never arrive. He orders servant after servant to check outside to see if the darkness is diminishing. Each time he is told that there is still darkness, the servant is sent to check again. When he can take the waiting no longer a messenger is dispatched to get the magician and is instructed to return at the greatest possible speed.

When the magician hears the emperor's decision, he shows no surprise. This stuns the younger man. When questioned about his lack of response, pointing to a window, the elder says, "Look, My Lord, it is still night outside. For what other reason would you have need of me? You look as though you have not slept a wink. That means you are more than just interested in my proposal!"

Paheni tells Haknobee that he is very observant and wise.

Now he feels more confident that this wise gentleman really has the solution to change his life for the better.

The two men spend the rest of the night discussing how and when to set the actual process in motion, then ending with a vow of secrecy.

By daybreak the plan is ready.

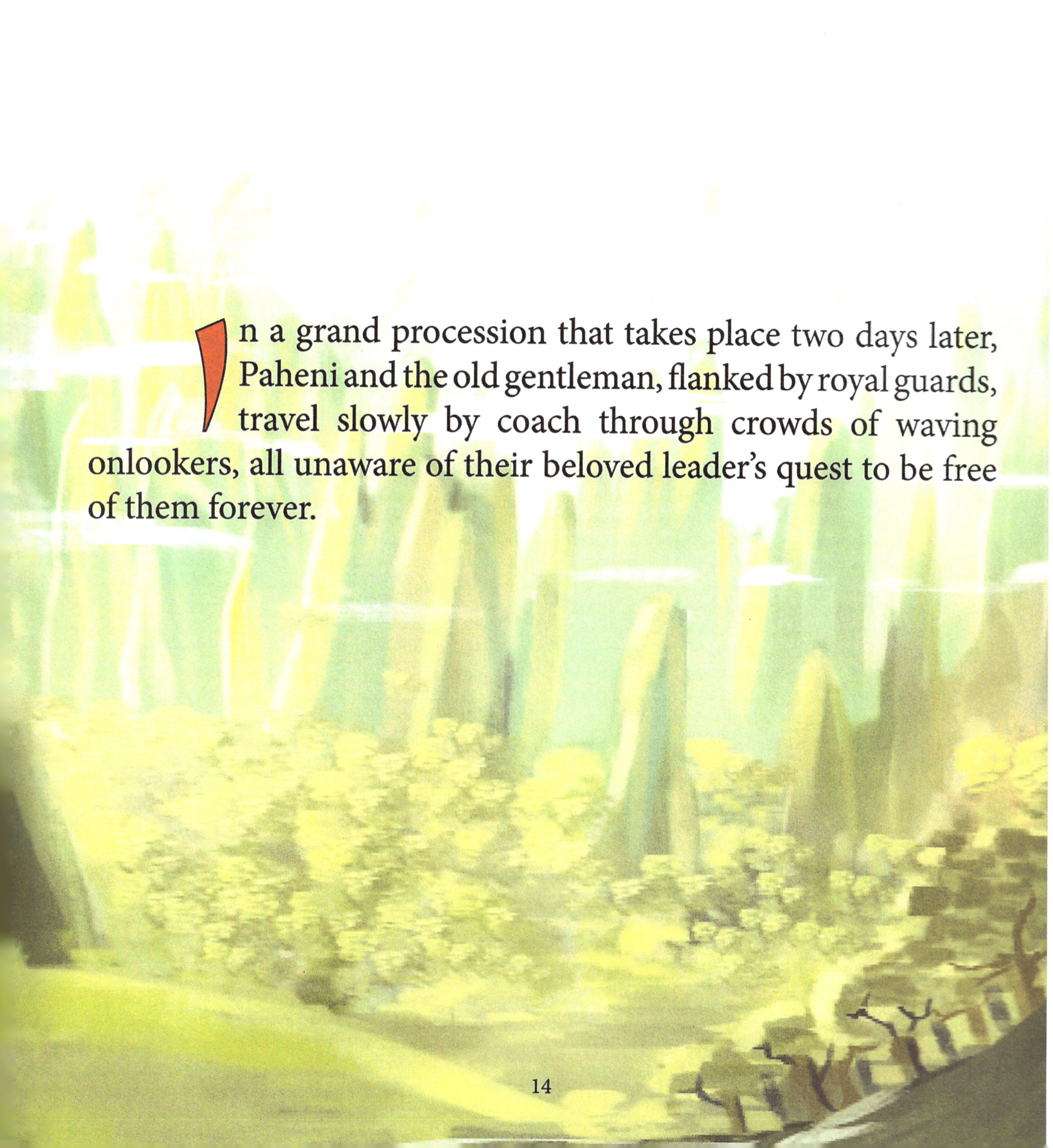

In a grand procession that takes place two days later, Paheni and the old gentleman, flanked by royal guards, travel slowly by coach through crowds of waving onlookers, all unaware of their beloved leader's quest to be free of them forever.

The caravan of travelers pass by village after village for a day and a half in route to a location in the rainforest that only the old man knows.

Weary and filled with great anxiety, the emperor begins to ask for more details about what is to take place once they reach their destination. "Will you use words or will you have to do something extraordinary to accomplish your magic? And during the ceremony will there be any discomfort?"

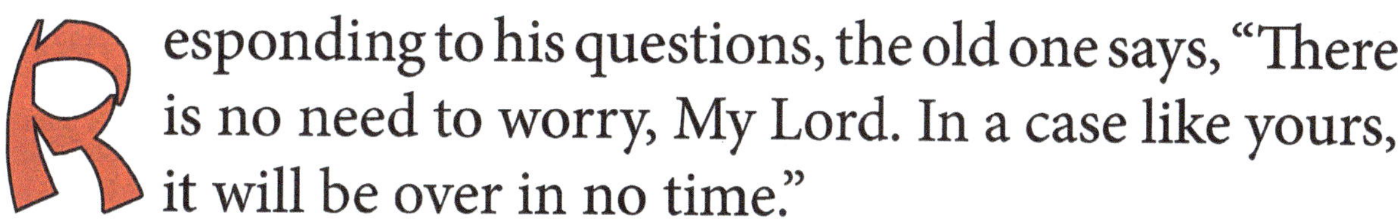

esponding to his questions, the old one says, "There is no need to worry, My Lord. In a case like yours, it will be over in no time."

The emperor not totally convinced, now asks, "What if the bird will not agree to any of this, what then?"

"Well Sire, first we must try to find that parrot. The place where he was last seen is the most dense and overgrown area in the jungle," the old man responds.

The emperor becomes very quiet after that, so much so, Haknobee turns to look at him. When he realizes that Paheni is sleeping, he tells the driver to make haste before dusk or they will have to stay overnight in the rainforest.

That really gets the caravan moving at a faster pace.

Paheni slowly opens his eyes just as they are pulling into a clearing at the edge of a large patch of old trees supporting tangled vines and hanging moss.

"What is this?" he asks, not fully awake, but after hearing animal noises and the rustling of trees coming from inside the forest, it does not take long for him to figure out where they are and what's happening. Anxiously, he says, "Oh, we've finally arrived! Now, where do we go from here?"

Haknobee, keenly aware of being watched by hundreds of eyes surrounding them, tells Paheni that only the two of them should go deeper into the thick forest in search of the parrot. He explains that if more than that were to go in, the inhabitants including the one they were looking for, may attack them or be frightened off. Then they would probably never get another opportunity to carry out the only solution to his dilemma.

The emperor looks around nervously, then insists upon taking along one of the guards. "Surely, there will be a need for more protection deeper in the interior," he says.

Honoring the emperor's demand, Haknobee orders one guard to join them, then speaks no more to the emperor for a while. It is obvious to him that the younger man overlooks his ability to protect them. However, his concerns now, must be to find the bird, make good his promise to the emperor, then head post haste in the direction of the castle before nightfall.

Their trek through the forest is not without some unpleasantness. Small broad-leafed plants, ferns, and a maze of small tree roots and fallen branches make their travel a bit tricky. Trying to see through the thick haze covering the interior proves to be difficult. The murky dimness makes it hard for the men to identify animals, especially birds that live high up in the understory of the forest.

While Paheni thinks to himself that the search for the parrot is becoming more of an effort than he expected, he wants to continue his quest. He remains hopeful that soon he will experience the feeling of being carefree in paradise.

The elder stops suddenly when he notices the faint outline of a brightly colored bird perched on the branch of a very tall tree. There is something in the bird's manner that reminds him of the one he had encountered months earlier.

When the elder calls out to him, the parrot recognizes his voice straight away and flies down just close enough to inquire, "What is your purpose for returning to this area again, so soon, sir?"

Extending a hand toward Paheni, the elder says, "This is My Lord, our exalted emperor," then pointing to the guard, he says, "and this is one of My Lord's royal guards. We did not come to do any harm, but we do have a proposition that may be of great interest to you. It could be the solution to getting what you think will bring you the most contentment in life."

The bird moves closer to hear more. His interest grows as Haknobee continues to speak.

Haknobee recounts their last conversation, then tells the parrot of the emperor's desire to switch places with him.

Having difficulty believing what he is hearing, the parrot says, "Please repeat that again, sir!"

"My Lord wishes to change places with you. You will become the ruler of his kingdom and he will become you, just a parrot in this very rainforest," the old gentleman repeats.

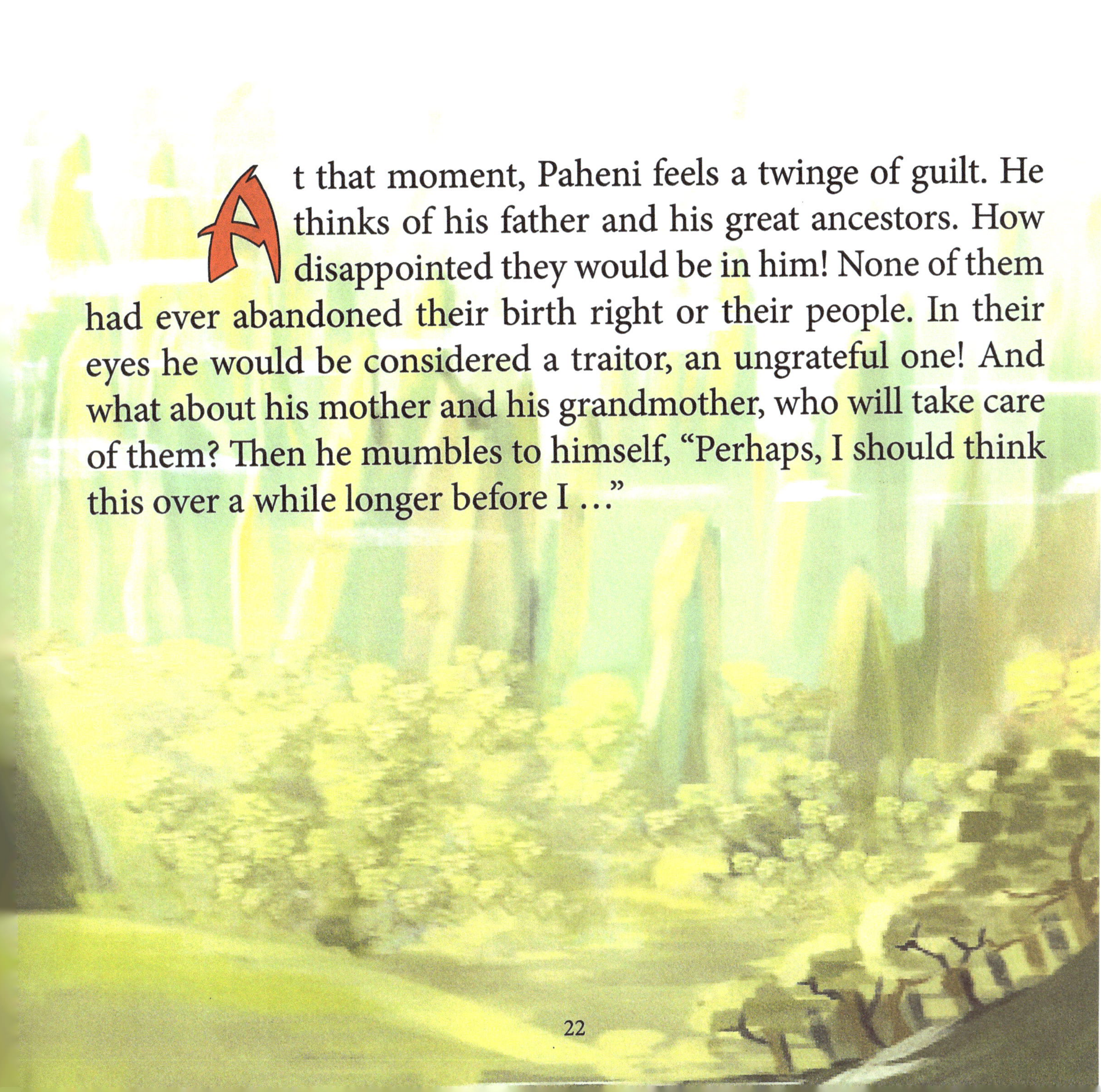

At that moment, Paheni feels a twinge of guilt. He thinks of his father and his great ancestors. How disappointed they would be in him! None of them had ever abandoned their birth right or their people. In their eyes he would be considered a traitor, an ungrateful one! And what about his mother and his grandmother, who will take care of them? Then he mumbles to himself, "Perhaps, I should think this over a while longer before I …"

ithout warning, a powerful voice is heard saying, "Now that both of you in my presence have made known your desires to switch lives, the deed is done!"

A resident of the rainforest now, Paheni is left sitting high up in the very same fruit tree where the bird was first spotted by Haknobee. He watches the caravan as it leaves with the new emperor. What a relief he feels knowing he doesn't have to stumble back through the prickly shrubs and the tangled web of tree roots again! This is his home now, and he is able to fly whenever and wherever he wishes. To himself he thinks, what a life!

Too tired to think of satisfying the hunger he is feeling, the parrot falls asleep right there on the branch.

Awaken suddenly by shrilled shrieks and screams that get louder and louder, the bird realizes it's a warning that danger is near by. After flying to a higher branch, he looks around to see what is causing such commotion and spots a giant of a snake already midway up the tree.

The bird is terrified when he sees how close he came to being snatched up and eaten by the snake. He quickly follows the other birds to another location.

nfortunately, as they settle in, a heavy downpour forces a horde of pesky insects to seek refuge in the same tree. Big trouble starts when the insects begin to view the birds as their source of food. The painful bites cause the flock such misery they seek yet another place to roost, but is unable to find one. Every suitable tree in the forest has already been claimed by other animals. And of course, they dare not try the upper canopy where eagles and hawks are among predators just waiting to ambush them.

With no place else to go, the parrot and the others return to the tree and continue to fight with their unwanted guests.

Unfamiliar with the long rainy seasons of the rainforest, the parrot is hopeful the intruding parasites will soon leave in search of other hosts, when it all ends!

Before the veil of darkness descends, the parrot enjoys a rare, quiet moment. During this time, he thinks about his past life as an emperor and the consequences of his decision to seek a more carefree existence. Feeling a bit sorry for himself, he says, "If only I had another chance, I would…." Loud growling from below interrupts his train of thought.

As the growling escalates, piercing shrieks and screams get the attention of every animal in hearing distance. Troupes of monkeys go into a frenzy making high pitched sounds as they leap dangerously from tree to tree.

Looking down, the parrot notices the outline of a tremendous animal prowling around the edge of the area. When he recognizes it as a leopard, he realizes why the monkeys are so wildly agitated.

In the midst of all the confusion, one monkey loses its footing and falls to the forest floor. After the dead animal is dragged off by the big cat, the community of animals calm down. But the parrot can not get the incident out of his mind. Even though he knows what happened there is nature's way of providing for one of its creatures in the wild, he doesn't want to ever witness such viciousness again!

What was he thinking? This is not a carefree life at all! One must be on watch at all times because danger is ever present. How he regrets his decision to come here! "I don't have the slightest idea what to do about my situation, but I know now, this is the wrong place for me! Perhaps, tomorrow I will come up with something," the parrot whispers faintly before falling into a troubled sleep.

The next morning, what sounds like human voices are heard in the distance. The animals, including the parrot, prepare to hide in case there is some real danger. As the voices get closer, the parrot clearly hears his old name being called. Immediately he responds by saying, "Who wants Paheni?"

A familiar voice answers, "Have you had enough carefree living, My Lord? Are you ready to come home?"

The bird thinks he is dreaming, but says, in case he is not, "Just get on with the magic as quickly as possible!"

Haknobee says in a loud, powerful voice, "Another is returning to the kingdom, now there are two. The magic is done!"

Paheni has so many questions to ask and so much to tell, but doesn't know where to start. Even though it is suggested that he saves his strength to travel back to the coach, the emperor manages to ask about the other parrot and how is it the elder knew he wanted to return to his former life.

aknobee explains that the parrot was once a farmer in his kingdom. He also wanted the carefree life, but all he has gotten so far is disappointment. But unlike Paheni, he's still searching. Then the old gentleman says, "I knew you would regret your decision, but some things you have to experience for yourself in order to grow and to be able to make better decisions in the future."

"And My Lord, I will continue to use my magical powers to keep you safe and to do what is best for our kingdom!"

The elder just wants to get the emperor back to his palace so he can be fed and looked after properly.

Looking at Paheni closely, the elder whispers to the guard with him, "His appearance is a fright, not at all as it was two days ago! What has happened to him? I'm really glad we returned for him earlier than planned. What would have become of him!"

Once the emperor is made comfortable inside the royal coach, he tells of his experience living in the rainforest as a parrot. It pains the old one to hear the horrid details, but he listens until the younger man falls asleep. He hopes that the harshness endured by Paheni in the wild will now cause him to accept and to appreciate the life he was born to.

oftly to himself, the elder says, "Perhaps, he has learned that running away from a problem is really not a solution and that some situations are not all they appear to be."

Haknobee strongly believes, because of the ordeal, the emperor will be a stronger and a wiser leader; one in whom his ancestors would be proud.

The trip back to the palace seems endless to Paheni. He can hardly wait to see the old place again. Feeling as though he has been away too long, he is anxious to get back to the safe, familiar surroundings of his childhood.

When the coach slows suddenly, Paheni knows the long journey is almost over. It is very hard for him to contain his excitement. Immediately he says, "I must take a walk through the palace gardens!"

Remembering the emperor's exhausted condition, the elder quickly responds, "My Lord, there will be plenty of time to take in the beauty of your gardens. Right now, you require rest if you intend to resume your royal duties tomorrow."

How wonderful those words sound to Paheni! He is more than ready. He knows the elder is right and is only looking out for his best interest. "You are right, my faithful friend. I have gained so much from your friendship and your great wisdom. It is now my time to show you my gratitude!" he says smiling happily.

nd that, the emperor does by appointing Haknobee his Senior Royal Advisor.

From that day forward, life for the emperor and his kingdom can only be described as

M-A-G-I-C-A-L!

The End